Love Shouts and Whispers

By the same author
The Clever Potato

Love Shouts and Whispers

Poems by Vernon Scannell

Illustrations by Tony Ross

Hutchinson

London   Sydney   Auckland   Johannesburg

A few more for Emma Kilcoyne

First published in Great Britain in 1990 by
Hutchinson Children's Books
An imprint of The Random Century Group Ltd
20 Vauxhall Bridge Road,
London SW1V 2SA

Random Century Australia (Pty) Ltd
88–91 Albion Street, Surry Hills, NSW 2010

Random Century New Zealand Limited
32–34 View Road, PO Box 40-086, Glenfield, Auckland 10

Random Century South Africa (Pty) Ltd
PO Box 337, Bergvei, South Africa

Photoset by Deltatype Ltd, Ellesmere Port
Printed and bound in Great Britain by
Butler and Tanner Ltd, Frome and London

British Library Cataloguing in Publication Data

Scannell, Vernon, 1922–
  Love shouts and whispers.
  I. Title   II. Ross, Tony, 1938–
  821.914

ISBN 0–09–174365–6

Contents

Note   None of the above poems have been previously published apart from the following: 'Growing Pain', 'Thelma', 'Poem for Jane' and 'Incendiary'.

Love-light

A taper lit in sunlight,
Pale yellow leaf of flame,
An upturned heart that trembled
As soft winds breathed your name,
Its brightness was diluted;
But, when the darkness came,
It shone with such pure brilliance
As put the stars to shame.

Why

They ask me why I love my love. I say,
'Why do summer's roses smell so sweet
And punctually put on their rich display?

'Why does winter lash the fields with sleet
And make cold music in the leafless trees
Yet strangely seem to warm our snug retreat?

'Why does moody April taunt and tease
With alternating sun and dancing rain?
Why do nettles sting the flesh like bees?

'Why are the stars tonight like silver grain
Broadcast on the far dark fields of sky?
Why does the owl rehearse its sad refrain?

'With loving, too: no point in asking why.
There is no answer.' That is my reply.

Love

Is it like a carnival with spangles and balloons,
Fancy-dress and comic masks and sun-drenched
    afternoons
Without a cloud to spoil the blue perfection of the
    skies?
*'Well yes, at first, but later on it might seem
    otherwise.'*

Is it like a summer night when stock and roses
    stain
The silken dark with fragrance and the nightingale
    again
Sweetly pierces silence with its silver blades of
    song?
*'I say once more it can be thus, but not for very
    long.'*

Is it like a great parade with drums and marching
  feet
And everybody cheering them, and dancing in the
  street,
With laughter swirling all around and only tears of
  joy?
*'If that alone, you'd find the fun would soon begin to
  cloy.'*

Is it like the falling snow, noiseless through the
  night;
Mysterious as moonlight and innocent and bright,
Changing the familiar world with its hypnotic spell?
*'It has been known to be like that, and other things
  as well.*

*'But if you find, when all the brightest ribbons have
  grown frayed,*
*The colours faded; music dumb, and all that great
  parade*
*Dismissed into the darkness where the moon has
  been put out,*
*Together you find warmth and strength, then that's
  what it's about.'*

The Power of Love

It can alter things:
The stormy scowl can become
Suddenly a smile.

The knuckly bunched fist
May open like a flower,
Tender a caress.

Beneath its bright warmth
Black ice of suspicion melts;
Danger is dazzled.

A plain and dull face
Astounds with its radiance
And sudden beauty.

Ordinary things —
Teacups, spoons and sugar-lumps —
Become magical.

The locked door opens;
Inside are leaves and moonlight;
You are welcomed in.

Its delicate strength
Can lift the heaviest heart
And snap hostile steel.

It gives eloquence
To the dumb tongue, makes plain speech
Blaze like poetry.

Grannie

I stayed with her when I was six then went
To live elsewhere when I was eight years old.
For ages I remembered her faint scent
Of lavender, the way she'd never scold
No matter what I'd done, and most of all
The way her smile seemed, somehow, to enfold
My whole world like a warm, protective shawl.

I knew that I was safe when she was near,
She was so tall, so wide, so large, she would
Stand mountainous between me and my fear,
Yet oh, so gentle, and she understood
Every hope and dream I ever had.
She praised me lavishly when I was good,
But never punished me when I was bad.

Years later war broke out and I became
A soldier and was wounded while in France.
Back home in hospital, still very lame,
I realized suddenly that circumstance
Had brought me close to that small town where she
Was living still. And so I seized the chance
To write and ask if she could visit me.

She came. And I still vividly recall
The shock that I received when she appeared
That dark cold day. Huge grannie was so small!
A tiny, frail, old lady. It was weird.
She hobbled through the ward to where I lay
And drew quite close and, hesitating, peered.
And then she smiled: and love lit up the day.

Dear You . . .

L ast time we met I wanted
O h, so much, to say,
V ery simply, how I felt
E xcited all that day.

L ong after you had left,
E ven late at night,
T he memory of your smiling face
T antalized my sight.
E very word I write is true:
R ead this slowly: I love you.

Contradictions of Love

As fragile as the eggshell bauble
    On a Christmas tree,
But durable as gleaming steel
    Of knife, or sword, or key.

Sweet as the fragrance of the rose
    Or honey from the bee,
But cold and scentless as the snow,
    And salty as the sea.

As gentle as a summer breeze
    Or mother's lullaby,
But burly as a hurricane
    Or thunder in the sky.

As magical as witches' spells
    Or blackbirds in a pie,
But plain and simple as good bread,
    Without which we would die.

Unspoken Love

I hear such regal music in my head,
Yet can't transmit to you a single bar:
I cannot sing, must speak to you instead.

But words, too, may be better left unsaid:
So difficult to speak when, from afar,
I hear such regal music in my head.

It is the light your loveliness has shed
Translated into sound; but what you are
I cannot sing, must speak to you instead.

Tonight's dark thunder might engender dread,
But I feel joy that no black wind can mar;
I hear such regal music in my head.

Ironic that my loving you has led
Me here, a troubadour without guitar:
I cannot sing, must speak to you instead.

Beneath your window as you lie in bed –
A silent nightingale, a shrouded star –
I hear such regal music in my head
But cannot sing, must speak to you instead.

Epitaph for a Gifted Man

He was not known among his friends for wit;
He owned no wealth, nor did he crave for it.
His looks would never draw a second glance;
He could not play an instrument or dance,
Or sing, or paint, nor would he ever write
The music, plays, or poems that delight
And win the whole world's worship and applause.
He did not fight for any noble cause;
Showed neither great extravagance nor thrift;
But he loved greatly: that was his one gift.

Growing Pain

The boy was barely five years old.
We sent him to the little school
And left him there to learn the names
Of flowers in jam jars on the sill
And learn to do as he was told.
He seemed quite happy there until
Three weeks afterwards, at night,
The darkness whimpered in his room.
I went upstairs, switched on his light,
And found him wide awake, distraught,
Sheets mangled and his eiderdown
Untidy carpet on the floor.
I said, 'Why can't you sleep? A pain?'
He snuffled, gave a little moan,
And then he spoke a single word:
'Jessica.' The sound was blurred.
'Jessica? What do you mean?'
'A girl at school called Jessica,
She hurts –' he touched himself between
The heart and stomach '– she has been
Aching here and I can see her.'
Nothing I had read or heard
Instructed me in what to do.
I covered him and stroked his head.
'The pain will go, in time,' I said.

Thelma

Thelma was a Brownie.
I never spoke to her
Although we spent a year together
In Standard Three.
I once followed her home
From the Brownie HQ.
There was honeysuckle in the gardens;
Songs of gramophones, too.
The satchel she brought to school
Was made of expensive leather
And in her hair
She wore a slide of tortoiseshell.
We never spoke,
Not once in all that time.
It was a long spell
And is not over:
When I smell honeysuckle now
It is Thelma I smell.

A Love Song

Even the vastness of the skies will lack
Space for this love, and send it back,
Sliding down the velvet night,
A meteor, a golden light,
A silent music falling.

At dawn, transformed to dew, it clings
To leaf and petal, then it sings
Through the throats of waking birds,
Steals meaning from all other words
Except your name, my darling.

Self-love

I love me very much,
I know I always shall;
I never find me boring;
I am my own best pal.

I'll never let me down
The way that others do;
I shall ignore all rivals;
I'll stick to me like glue.

When other people moan
That life gets worse and worse,
I gaze into the mirror
At Mr Universe

Who smiles and nods at me;
We both know what is meant:
'How could such faithful lovers
Fail to be content?'

And yet I must confess
At times I feel a touch
Perplexed that other people
Don't love me just as much.

And, when the lights go out
And looking-glasses wear
Cloaks of starless darkness,
However hard I stare

I see no answering gaze
And, cold as steel or stone,
Looms the bitter knowledge
That I am quite alone.

Lullaby

For Nancy, aged two

The house is silent.
Black-furred night is heaped against the window,
And one pale, luminous eye remarks
How slowly hours devour the light.
Sleep softly darling;
I shall keep three candles lit beside your bed,
Three golden blades will pierce the heart
Of night till morning finds him dead;
Sleep softly darling, sleep.

The Headmaster's Song

I'm mad about Muriel Murgatroyd
    Who joined the staff in May.
My concentration's been destroyed;
    I think of her all day.

She teaches Art, and I'm the kind
    Of man who just can't see
What art is all about; I find
    It bores or puzzles me.

Yet *she's* a work of art all right;
    No sculpture or fine painting
Could possibly delight my sight
    And bring me close to fainting,

As really happened when she came
    To Bugton Comprehensive;
And even now, to hear her name
    Makes me grow vague and pensive.

I'm single, but I'm no great catch;
    Not handsome, far from youthful;
Miss M and I don't make a match
    I grant, if I am truthful.

But I am free to dream. The kids
    Would never guess that nightly
Miss M and I, behind closed lids,
    Are clasped together tightly.

The Policeman's Song

I am the guardian of the law;
I pound my daily beat.
You'll see me go, majestic, slow,
On my enormous feet.

My face beneath the helmet brim
Looks serious and stern;
You'd never guess that in my breast
Flames of passion burn.

I keep my lips together tight,
No hint of smile or grin,
Yet hear and feel warm music steal
Secretly within.

Until three weeks ago I thought
Of nothing but the job;
Then life was changed, all re-arranged
By WPC Cobb.

And so I pound my beat and hope
That when we're both off duty
I'll conquer doubt and ask her out,
Though dazzled by her beauty.

Her hair is gold, her eyes are blue,
My heart-beats skip and hop
To think that she might one day be
My very own fair cop.

The Pop Star's Song

O how I love you baby,
O baby you're just swell;
I love your eyes, they're magic;
You've got me in your spell.

I love you in the summer,
But baby I'll be there
When autumn leaves have shrivelled
And winter chills the air.

I'm crazy for you baby;
All the day and night
I dream of you in colour
As well as black-and-white.

O baby you're the music
Of heavenly guitars;
Your skin is soft as moonlight,
Your eyes shine like the stars.

I love you madly baby;
You know I really do.
I think you know the reason –
I'm a baby too!

I'm a drooling baby,
And you don't mind a bit;
I yowl and howl in public
And I get paid for it!

So baby let's get married
And one day there might be
With luck another baby
As fortunate as me.

The Sailor's Song

The north wind howls, the swollen seas
Crash on the deck like falling trees;
Ice rattles like a jailer's keys,
But I defy the weather;
My thoughts spin round a single theme;
In freezing dark I see the gleam
Of my dear sweetheart's eyes and dream
Of her and me together.

She is my star by which I steer;
All through the eight-bell watch I hear
The chiming of her name as clear
As snowflake on a raven;
She is my sextant and my chart;
The calculations of the heart
Assure me we shall never part
Once I have reached my haven.

My final voyage, and after this
I'll settle down and never miss
The waltzing waves and salty kiss
Thrown from the flirting ocean;
Instead of shanties I shall sing
Lilting love-songs as I bring
My promise with a golden ring
Of strong sea-deep devotion.

So goodbye skipper, bosun, mate,
And come on lads, let's celebrate
Once we're ashore and congregate
For one last tot at Harwich;
I can't stay long, I'll have to go,
Then no more rum and yo-ho-ho;
I'm going to berth where no gales blow,
In the sheltered bay of marriage.

Miss Steeples

Miss Steeples sat close;
She touched me.
Her hands were white,
Fingernails pink,
Like shells of prawns.
They tapped my desk
And, as she murmured,
Numbers blurred.
She smelled of spring
And cool cash chemists.
One summer evening,
Not by chance,
I met her walking
Near the green
Tennis-court
She beautified
Dressed in white.
In one hand swung
A netted catch
Of tennis balls.
She smiled and said,
'Hello.'
She smiled.
Love-punctured
I could not answer.
At the end of the summer
She went away.
It was her smell I loved
And her fingernails.

Poem for Jane

So many catalogues have been
Compiled by poets, good and bad,
Of qualities that they would wish
To see their infant daughters wear;
Or lacking children they have clad
Others' daughters in the bright
Imagined garments of the flesh,
Prayed for jet or golden hair
Or for the inconspicuous
Homespun of the character
That no one ever whistles after.
Dear Jane, whatever I may say
I'm sure approving whistles will
Send you like an admiral on
Ships of welcome in a bay
Of tender waters where the fish
Will surface longing to be meshed
Among the treasures of your hair.
And as for other qualities
There's only one I really wish
To see you amply manifest
And that's a deep capacity
For loving; and I long for this
Not for any lucky one
Who chances under your love's sun
But because, without it, you
Would never know completely joy
As I know joy through loving you.

Love Rhymes

Love, as any poet knows,
Owns few pure rhymes to chime with it;
This does not mean that only prose
Can take the word and climb with it
To peaks of celebration or despair.
What are the rhymes? Well, *glove* and *shove*,
The gentle *dove*, aloof *above*;
And that's the lot as far as I'm aware.

Some silly teachers speak about
'Eye-rhymes' for *love*, like *rove* and *move*.
Ignore them. Throw such notions out!
They're nonsense and they only prove
Their advocates to be quite deaf to rhyme,
Which must be heard and cannot be
Recognized by sight, as we
Cannot see the scent of rose or thyme.

And I am fairly sure this dearth
Of words to rhyme with *love* somehow
Increases what the word is worth –
Though why that shortage should endow
This greater value I can't explicate.
I only know that *love* should be
In verse or life used sparingly
In case its power and beauty dissipate.

The Meaning of Love

I love liquorice and I love pop;
I love the smell in the baker's shop.
I love Tennyson, our tabby cat;
I love chips in sizzling fat.
I love roundabouts, dodgems, slides;
I love the seaside – donkey-rides,
Sticks of rock and salty smells.
I love the sound of distant bells
Carried by summer's evening breeze
Over the fields, above the trees,
Tumbling in the trembling air.
I love Parkinson's mournful stare
(He's my spaniel and not very bright);
I love the stars on a frosty night,
The first snow of winter's dazzling white.
I love the spring when the daffodils
And blossoming branches bless the hills
And valleys where bright glitter and gleam
Of rustling sunlit waters seem
Reflections of the birds' delight
In their melodious, wheeling flight.
I love the sound of the bass guitar,
The pungent whiff of bubbling tar –
But wait a second! Now I find
All this time I've been deaf and blind
To what 'love' really means. You see,
The things I've listed here might be
Enjoyable and dear to me;
But *love* them? No, that's not quite true.

We shouldn't say it, though we do.
Love is something different:
It's magical, will re-invent
Yourself and all the world you know;
You don't need me to tell you so.
Of course we'll go on just the same
Using 'love' when we wish to name
The things we like and find are fun —
Hot cheese-burger or hot-cross-bun,
Tennis, football, crisp french fries —
But when we think of the smiling eyes
Of him or her we idolise,
We use the word in its proper sense,
And that little syllable holds immense
Power beyond all measuring;
Whether we whisper it, shout or sing,
It means no less than everything.

Words from the
Father of the Bride

They tell you love lasts forever
Like a wedding-ring's golden gleam
Going round and round the finger,
But this is just a dream
Deceiving the eye and the ear,
So don't you believe them, sweetheart;
Don't you believe them, dear.

They tell you his vows and pledges
Will never turn out to be false,
That life with your love will always
Swirl bright like an endless waltz
With only soft music to hear;
But don't you believe them, sweetheart;
Don't you believe them dear.

They tell you the final chapter
Must end with the formal kiss
Of bride and groom at the altar,
Guarantee of perfect bliss
For year after magical year;
But don't you believe them, sweetheart;
Don't you believe them, dear.

That's not the last chapter, darling;
There's another volume to come
With scenes that would shock your auntie
And bring tears to the eyes of your mum.
When they tell you there's nothing to fear,
Don't you believe them, sweetheart;
Don't you believe them, dear.

Ah, precious, there's no need for crying;
Forgive me and dry those sad eyes;
The venomous things I've been saying
Will all turn out to be lies.
It's loss of your love that I fear;
So don't you believe *me*, sweetheart;
Don't you believe *me*, dear.

Famous Lovers

Everyone has heard about
Romeo and Juliet,
And all those lovers long ago
We modern sweethearts can't forget.

Since you and I first fell in love
I've thought a lot about the old
Tales of famous couples whose
Stories are inscribed in gold.

I really mean in golden words
That please the heart and mind and ear,
Prose and poetry that tell
Of Launcelot and Guinevere,

Of Heloise and Abelard,
Tristram and Iseult: such names,
As Dido and Aneas, gleam
And flicker in the dark like flames.

Mind you, their owners seemed to come
To sticky ends. Maybe it's wise
For us to stay anonymous
And hidden from the public's eyes.

Though, come to think of it, I can't
Imagine that our names would be
Engraved eternally upon
The universal memory.

Kev and Tracey? I don't see
A poem here, I must confess,
Or a play. But don't think this
Is proof we love each other less.

43

The Puzzle

I didn't used to think that I was vain,
But now, perhaps, I'd better think again.
I'll tell you why. Three weeks ago today
My friend – well, maybe I had better say
My friend-that-was, Lee Anderson's his name –
He and I had gone out for a game
Of tennis which was then our current craze.
We'd just begun the summer holidays.
Anyway, we'd reached the final set
When I first saw that face I can't forget.
A girl, quite on her own, was standing there
And watching us. She seemed to have an air
Of slight amusement; not a bit impressed,
And yet I saw a kind of interest
In those bright, smiling eyes. I wouldn't call
Her beautiful; she wasn't short or tall,
Just medium I suppose; and though her looks
Were not the kind you read about in books,
Or see on video or film, they struck
Right to my heart. I felt it lurch and buck.
I won that final set quite easily
And as we left the court I saw that she
Had walked away, but not so quickly that
We could not catch her up and maybe chat
Her up as well. And that is what we did.
Lee said little, so I made my bid
With confidence and asked her for a date.
She paused, then said, 'But what about your
    mate?'

I said, 'Two's company, the saying goes.'
Lee smiled. 'My name is Lee.' She said, 'Mine's
    Rose.'
And suddenly I knew that she preferred
My friend to me. I didn't say a word
But turned, strode off, trying to look cool,
But now, I realize, looking like a fool.
And here's the thing that goes on puzzling me:
Lee is small and rather weedy. He
Is nothing much to look at. Why did she
Fancy him in preference to me?
And yet she did, and this I can't deny.
Perhaps one day someone will tell me why.

Love Words

'Karen Blake loves Trevor Clark,'
So it says on the wall above
The seat in the shelter in the park;
I like to think that she will love
Trevor forever, in light and dark,
In heat and cold, all kinds of weather;
She'll love him in silk and love him in leather.

But what about Trevor? It doesn't say
If he loves Karen. We can't tell.
For all we know he'd rather stay
Out of love's sweet prison-cell
Where you are haunted night and day
By fears that you may lose your darling,
Your dark night's lamp, your shimmering starling.

Another thought occurs to me:
Maybe Trevor doesn't know
Karen Blake at all, though she
Has watched him walking to and fro
From her window, secretly,
Content at first to steal these fleeting
Glimpses, dreaming of a meeting.

Perhaps she grew impatient. Then
One early night slipped out to scrawl
With her purple felt-tipped pen
Those words upon the shelter-wall.
You wonder why? Well, certain men
And women, too, believe they're able
To change the world however stable:

They maintain that words possess
Magic powers, and Karen might
Have thought so too. It's just a guess
But maybe she went out that night
Resolved quite simply to confess
Her secret love, perhaps believing
The verbal spell would prove worth weaving,

And Trevor in his heart would find
A chime of love that echoed hers.
Perhaps. But love, they say, is blind
And unpredictable, occurs
Explosively, is not designed;
Rejects control and even magic.
Its birth is lyric; its death is tragic.

So Karen, dear, don't feel despair
If Trevor doesn't love you back;
But if he does I hope you'll share
A lucky life that knows no lack
Of happiness though this I swear:
Should you wed one more tall and clever
Trevor will live in your dreams forever.

Waiting for the Call

Sitting in the curtained room
Waiting for the distant call,
Hearing only darkness move
Almost noiseless in the hall
Where the telephone is hunched
Like a little cat whose purr
May be wakened if you press
Ear against its plastic fur,
He sits and knows the urgent noise
Probably will not occur:
There's little hope and, if it does,
He's sure – almost – it won't be her.

Cupboard Love

Julia was eight years old.
Her mother baked, then iced a cake
With candles and, inscribed in gold,
The figure 'eight' and Julia's name;
And to her party she asked Jake
And was delighted when he came.

She'd seen him only twice before;
In fact they'd not exchanged a word.
Jake's parents had moved in next door
A week ago, so this would be
The first occasion that occurred
To meet each other properly.

And what a fine occasion too!
Julia wore her party dress,
New shoes and bracelet, also new;
And candlelight gleamed on the spread
Of sandwiches of egg and cress,
Bright jelly, buns and gingerbread.

Then, after tea and various games
Julia said, 'I know, let's play
Hide and Seek! Put all our names
Inside a hat and draw to see
Who will be the seeker. They
All asked themselves who it would be.

And soon they knew – a boy named Dean.
Julia was pleased to find
That neither she nor Jake had been
The one to search, and so she spied
On Jake when Dean was left behind
And all the others went to hide.

She followed Jake who did not know
The layout of the house. She said,
'I know the perfect place to go.
Come with me. I'll show you where
We can hide.' And then she led
The way up to the attic stair.

At the foot and hard to see
In the shadows was a door.
Julia whispered, 'Follow me.'
She opened it and went inside
A cupboard large enough for four.
Jake entered after his small guide.

The door half-closed, they stood quite still
In silent darkness. Minutes passed,
Then she reached out her hand until
It found his own and slowly their
Fingers twined and then held fast.
How long? She did not know or care.

Julia is fourteen now.
She tells her mum she doesn't know
What presents she received or how
Many children came or who
Was at that party long ago –
Though what she says is not quite true.

Jake's family has moved away
To somewhere on the continent.
Does he recall that distant day,
She wonders, or does she alone
Find it lingers like a scent,
And has a flavour all its own?

Incendiary

That one small boy with a face like pallid cheese
And burnt-out little eyes could make a blaze
As brazen, fierce and huge, as red and gold
And zany yellow as the one that spoiled
Three thousand guinea's worth of property
And crops at Godwin's Farm on Saturday
Is frightening – as fact and metaphor:
An ordinary match intended for
The lighting of a pipe or kitchen fire
Misused may set a whole menagerie
Of flame-fanged tigers roaring hungrily.
And frightening, too, that one small boy should set
The sky on fire and choke the start to heat
Such skinny limbs and such a little heart
Which would have been content with one warm
    kiss
Had there been anyone to offer this.

Love Shouts and Whispers

Love shouts and whispers and it often sings,
And, even when the voice is hoarse or low,
It somehow manages to rise on wings
Of sweet and secret music and will grow
Lovelier as you listen through the years,
Though only audible to lovers' ears.

Love shouts out loud, exultant, in its youth,
And longs for all the world to recognize
That it may lead towards the well of truth
And lasting happiness if we are wise
And trust the compass-bearings of the heart,
Discarding cautious reason's careful chart.

Love whispers in the autumn evening's calm
But, though the voice is soft, the words are bright
And durable as diamonds. No harm
Will come to lovers in the prowling night;
And when white winter shakes its icy chains
Love whispers warmth that comforts and sustains.

Waiting for Her

His feet are frozen lumps of meat.
The night wind scampers down the street
And like a naughty pup it nips
His nose and ears. Both burning lips
Are dry and cracked, and yet he stays,
Hands in pockets, and his gaze
Is fixed upon the softly lit
Curtained windows opposite.
He is not even sure that she
Is there at home. It might well be
That she is out with lucky friends,
Or worse, just one. This notion sends
A glinting pain into his heart,
Jealousy, the poison-dart
That causes fever of despair,
And self-dislike that's hard to bear.
And yet he would not be without
The hurt, excitement, hope and doubt
That keep him waiting in the night,
Longing for the brief delight
Of one quick glimpse of her to make
His world so warm you might mistake
It for the tropics filled with rich
Melody and fragrance which
Would send him dizzy with desire
And fill his veins with liquid fire.
But she does not appear. He knows
Only that the north wind blows,
And all his dreams of him and her

Could not, in waking life, occur,
For, even if he knew her name,
His hopeless state would stay the same,
And if she passed him standing there,
Hunched against the cruel air,
It's doubtful if she'd be aware
Of him at all. Why should she be
Since he is twelve years old and she
Is almost twice as old as he?

A Kind of Madness

Love is a kind of madness:
Or so some people claim.
It could be true: since I met you
Nothing's been the same.

I've grown quite absent-minded;
I wander in a dream
Through city streets and green retreats
Of hill and wood and stream.

I almost got run over
Crossing Spencer Place;
The driver swore but his wild roar
Could not erase your face.

When walking in the country
I speak to flowers and birds,
Though knowing well no one can tell
What love is like in words.

But nonetheless I sweeten
With your sweet name, the air,
And when stars light the halls of night
Again I breathe it there.

I laugh for no clear reason
And tap-dance in the rain;
If I am mad, then I am glad
And pity all the sane.

If love is a kind of madness
I hope no cure is found
To cancel this wild, soaring bliss
And dump me on dull ground.

59

Horror Film

Every week his parents gave
Him pocket money and he'd pay
For sweets and comics but he'd save
Enough to go each Saturday
To the movie matinée
Where the timid and the brave
Performed their deeds upon the screen
And in one memorable scene
Dainty ladies offered their
Involuntary gifts of blood.
A creature slunk towards its lair;
A strangled cat clawed at the mud;
A body in a coffin lay,
Soft conker in its satin case;
The candle flame was blown away,
But not before he saw the face
Staring through the dusty glass,
The fanged and slavering jaws agape,
The matted hair like withered grass,
That could not quite conceal the shape
Of almost human features, hide
The desperate appeal that cried
From self-accusing, frightened eyes.
The boy's own eyes were also wide
But not with fear; he recognized
Beneath the piteous brute disguise
The need for what might humanize:
The welcome or embrace that can
Change lonely monster into Man.

Something in Common

A summer afternoon: the warm sun leant
Its glimmering shafts from classroom windows
    while
Miss Markham's voice purred on, and Julie bent
Her head, so no one saw the secret smile
That touched her lips as she remembered how
John blushed and stammered when, at morning
    break,
At last he'd spoken. She was certain now:
He cared for her. He'd asked if he could take
Her out on Saturday, disco or
Perhaps a movie. She had blushed as well,
And stupidly stared down towards the floor;
And yet John liked her – somehow she could tell –
Just as much as she liked him.

                    And then
Her reverie was splintered by a voice
Calling out her name. Miss Markham spoke:
'And what in your opinion was the choice
Open to the King? Would he invoke
His sacred rights as monarch or bow down
Before the Commons' will?' Miss Markham's eyes
Were narrowed and her forehead wore a frown.
'Or do you think that he might compromise?'

Poor Julie's mind was blank. She had not heard
Anything of what had been explained.
She blinked and gulped but could not say a word.

Miss Markham snapped: 'You are a feather-brained
And lazy child. See me after school
And I shall give you extra work to do.'
Julie knew that she must look a fool
And, what was more, that she deserved it too.

Saturday arrived and she and John
Met, as they'd arranged, but did not go
To film or disco; both decided on
A country walk, so they could get to know
Each other better. They were rather shy
But not for long. They quickly found that they
Had such a lot in common time flew by,
Till Julie noticed, with surprised dismay,
The hour was late and it was time to turn
Back to town and head for home in case
Her parents were concerned and John might earn
Disfavour and be packed off in disgrace.

And so they hurried back towards the bright
City centre; it was there, outside
The Theatre Royal that a startling sight
Met Julie's eyes: Miss Markham, like a bride,
Was smiling as she walked beside a tall
Good-looking man and Julie was aware,
Amazed, the smile was meant for her, and all
At once she knew Miss Markham now would
    share
With her a bond, though neither of them would
Express in words what both had understood.

No Sense of Direction

I have always admired
Those who are sure
Which turning to take,
Who need no guide
Even in war
When thunders shake
The torn terrain,
When battalions of shrill
Stars all desert
And the derelict moon
Goes over the hill:
Eyes chained by the night
They find their way back
As if it were daylight.
Then, on peaceful walks
Over strange wooded ground,
They will find the right track,
Know which of the forks
Will lead to the inn
I would never have found;
For I lack their gift,
Possess almost no
Sense of direction.
And yet I owe
A debt to this lack,
A debt so vast
No reparation
Can ever be made,
For it led me away

From the road I sought
Which would carry me to –
I mistakenly thought –
My true destination:
It made me stray
To this lucky path
That ran like a fuse
And brought me to you
And love's bright, soundless
Detonation.

The Prisoner's Song

The stars that are whistling above the black town
Embroider the covers where lovers lie down,
Supplying sweet sanction for all that they do,
But glitter derision for me and for you.

The far train that calls like an owl in the night,
Runs straight as a fuse through the darkness to
    light,
Exploding in rendezvous, lucky ones who
In delight are united, unlike me and you.

The plane tipped with jewels of light at the wings
Sings loud in the clouds and indifferently brings
Exiles to firesides, the false to the true,
But mocks the cold distance between me and you.

Be patient my dearest, the night is in sight
When the stars and the plane and the train will
    unite
To heal separation and we shall be free
To relish the feast laid for you and for me.

Dark Lover

No need for tears because the night has come;
You have no cause to lie down with despair
Though voices of the sunlit hours are dumb
And darkness stains the song-forsaken air.
You must not hammer on the padlocked gate
Nor call out like a child who is afraid,
But let your fear and panic dissipate
And then accept this gift that night has made.

Drink deep of sleep and in your dreams behold
The golden lady of the afternoon
Extend her arms and smilingly enfold,
And be enfolded by, her Prince, and swoon,
As they together to his cave descend,
Dark lover without whom her life would end.

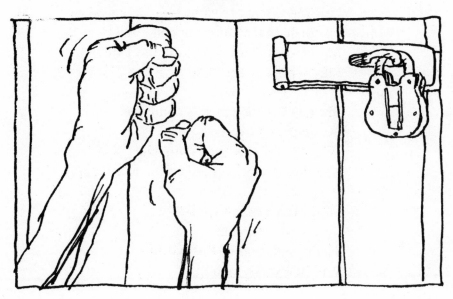

69

A New World

When I awoke this morning
Everything was changed;
All the world's green furniture
Somehow re-arranged.

The petals were all brighter;
Birdsong thrilled the air,
Silver sweet and jubilant;
Fragrance everywhere!

And I, who was so grumpy
And lazy as a rule,
Cheerfully jumped out of bed,
Keen to go to school;

Not for worthy reasons –
Or those that would impress
My teachers and my Mum and Dad –
Like scholarly success;

But just because there's someone
I cannot wait to see.
When I first saw that someone
The whole world changed for me.

We have not even spoken
But, if we ever do,
The population of this world
Will be exactly two!

The Most Precious Thing
A Jewish Folktale

A merchant lived in Sidon long ago
Who had been married for ten years or so,
Quite happily except for one sad thing –
Their silent home was never known to ring
With children's voices. We today might say
That this was not a tragedy, but they
Felt differently in that far time and place:
To have no heir was viewed as dark disgrace.

And so the husband went with heavy heart
To see the Rabbi and arrange to part
From his dear wife. The Rabbi sadly said,
'So be it. But remember, when you wed,
You held a splendid feast? Well, I commend
That you should also celebrate the end
Of your good marriage with another feast.
You owe that to your faithful wife at least.'

Before the feast began the merchant took
His wife aside and said to her, 'Now look,
I feel so guilty treating you this way.
You know I love you more than words can say,
Yet I must have a child. We've not been blessed,
So we must part. But you must choose the best,
Most precious thing in all the house before
You leave, and you may keep it evermore.'

She smiled her thanks. And when the feast began
She saw he drank more wine than anyone,
And very soon both he and darkness fell;
He drowned in sleep's unfathomable well.
When he awoke he did not recognize
The room in which he lay. To his surprise
His wife came in and kissed his puzzled brow
And said she hoped that he felt better now.

'Where am I?' he exclaimed. 'This room? This
    bed?'
'You're in my father's house,' she, smiling, said.
'I told the serving men to bring you here.
You said that I could take the thing most dear
And precious from the house. Well, that was you.
You are the dearest thing to me.' He knew
That moment that he could not part from this
Sweet loving wife, so he returned her kiss.

Then off they went to tell the Rabbi; he
Was glad to hear their news and so all three
Knelt and prayed to God that there would be
A child to make complete the couple's joy;
And in the following spring a healthy boy
Was born to them in answer to that prayer,
And happiness, like birdsong, filled the air
And made a second Eden blossom there.

Villanelle

You ask me if our present love will grow
More beautiful and strong as time goes by:
I cannot tell you what I do not know.

Perhaps love, like the sea, will ebb and flow —
But now I sense vague doubt and wonder why
You ask me if our present love will grow.

Are you afraid that soon the splendid glow
That we both felt at first will start to die?
I cannot tell you what I do not know.

I'm almost sure our love won't fade — although
I find I can't quite look you in the eye.
You ask me if our present love will grow,

And I begin to feel a cold wind blow
Where all before was warm; there's no reply:
I cannot tell you what I do not know.

We must hold firm to what we value so —
My darling, do not turn away and sigh!
You ask me if our present love will grow.
I cannot tell you what I do not know.

The Reward

I strode across the moors all day
And, only when the darkness came,
I whispered, like a prayer, her name;
But burly winds snatched it away.

I reached the city, but I found
No place to shelter, and again
I breathed her name but icy rain
Drenched and froze the fragile sound.

Next day I left the heartless town
And found an oak tree in a glade,
And carved her name with careful blade,
But great winds came and blew it down.

At last I lay, no roof above,
With one rough blanket of despair;
I heard a sigh, looked up, and there
She stood and smiled and said, 'My love . . .'

Secrets

I'm going to meet my sweetheart
    With a ribbon in my hair,
In taffeta and new red shoes –
    But I won't tell you where.

We might meet in the morning
    At eight, or nine, or ten,
Or when bright day has slipped away –
    But I won't tell you when.

He is not only handsome
    But brave and honest too;
He's kind and smart; he owns my heart –
    But I won't tell you who.

Though, if today he gives me
    That starry diamond ring,
Well, then I might, in my delight,
    Tell you everything.

The Young and Hopeful Lover

I knew that I would have to wait
    Years and years before
I carried, as my bride, Miss Hyde
    Through my own front door.

And I was quite prepared to wait
    Patiently until
I'd go away and then, one day,
    Come back all dressed to kill.

I mean I'd be in uniform –
    Para or *Marine* –
And I would wait outside the gate,
    Muscular and lean.

Miss Hyde would see me standing there
    As she came out of school;
She'd be wide-eyed as I would stride
    Towards her, smiling, cool.

But now I'm told she is engaged –
    And this you'd never guess –
To Mr Trench who teaches French!
    I'm shocked, I must confess.

I should have told her of my plans –
    Or so it now appears –
I think she would have understood
    And waited a few years.

Yet I've not given up all hope.
I still dream of the day
When I shall be grown up and free
To carry her away!